MADELINE
AND THE CATS OF ROME

Story and pictures by
John Bemelmans Marciano

VIKING

VIKING
Published by Penguin Group
Penguin Young Readers Group, 345 Hudson Street, New York, New York 10014, U.S.A.
Penguin Group (Canada), 90 Eglinton Avenue East, Suite 700, Toronto, Ontario, Canada M4P 2Y3
(a division of Pearson Penguin Canada Inc.)
Penguin Books Ltd, 80 Strand, London WC2R 0RL, England
Penguin Ireland, 25 St Stephen's Green, Dublin 2, Ireland (a division of Penguin Books Ltd)
Penguin Group (Australia), 250 Camberwell Road, Camberwell, Victoria 3124, Australia
(a division of Pearson Australia Group Pty Ltd)
Penguin Books India Pvt Ltd, 11 Community Centre, Panchsheel Park, New Delhi – 110 017, India
Penguin Group (NZ), 67 Apollo Drive, Rosedale, North Shore 0632, New Zealand
(a division of Pearson New Zealand Ltd.)
Penguin Books (South Africa) (Pty) Ltd, 24 Sturdee Avenue, Rosebank, Johannesburg 2196, South Africa

Penguin Books Ltd, Registered Offices: 80 Strand, London WC2R 0RL, England

First published in 2008 by Viking, a division of Penguin Young Readers Group

1 3 5 7 9 10 8 6 4 2

Copyright © John Bemelmans Marciano, 2008
All rights reserved

LIBRARY OF CONGRESS CATALOGING-IN-PUBLICATION DATA IS AVAILABLE
ISBN 978-0-670-06297-3

Manufactured in China
Set in Bodoni

MADELINE

AND THE CATS OF ROME

From an old house in Paris that was covered with vines
Left twelve little girls in two straight lines.
Their bags were packed, a camera stowed;
They were ready to escape the cold.

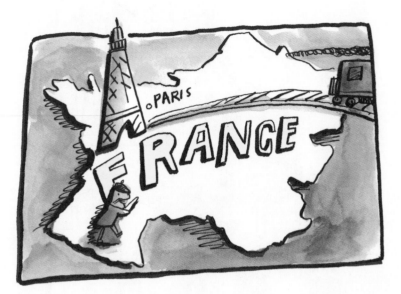

The train it leaves at half past nine—
Hurry, hurry, Madeline!
Across the Alps the pace was slow;
The mountains still were packed with snow.
But the far and farther south they traveled
The more that winter came unraveled.
Although it's dreary back at home,
The time has come for . . .

SPRING IN ROME!

Down the steps they took a stroll

Hearing bells of churches toll.

Here is a fountain they found quite appealing

And everyone loved the Sistine ceiling.
But in Italy the greatest treat

Comes when it is time to eat.

Miss Clavel said, "Over here, signore —

Twelve plates of pasta, per favore."

The hours of the day were running out.

The sun was setting, or just about.

"One last photo, let's press in tight."
Said Miss Clavel, "Yes, that's right."
But the moment she had her camera drawn

It was yanked from her hands by the strap and was gone!

Madeline took up the chase—

First a theft and now a race!

Into the fountain with a splash

Through the market in a dash

Across the river they kept the tail,
But coming back

They lost the trail.

Madeline said, "There is no justice—

That little thief completely lost us."

Just then a cat, seeking some affection,

Arched its back in Madeline's direction.

Madeline said, "My, what a nice kitten."

Her dog was of a different opinion.

"GENEVIEVE!" Madeline yelled—too late!
She had followed the cat through a locked-up grate
Into a house about to fall down,
Found in the poorest part of town.

Madeline pushed the door; it creaked.

"Is anyone there?" she asked as she peeked.

From somewhere deep in the shadowy dark

She heard Genevieve's whimpering bark.

Then Madeline saw, to her great surprise,

Those shining, staring, glaring . . .

EYES!

They were cats—cats!—look at them all!

There were cats on the sofa, cats in the hall,

Cats coming out of a hole in the wall!

A voice behind her, clear and strong, said,

"You have come where you don't belong."

Madeline turned in disbelief
To see that it was—"The camera thief!"

"Yes, 'tis I, the thief Caterina—
Protector of the Colonia Felina!

"We are the orphans of the street,
These cats and I.
So that we may eat is the reason why
I steal from you tourist passersby."

"While I applaud your charity,
Let me say this with clarity:
STEALING IS WRONG—no matter the cause.
You may not like it, but those are the laws."

"It is easy for you to judge and to scold—
For what do you know of hunger and cold?

"Here is your camera—now don't be slow.
Just take your well-groomed mutt and go!"
The two of them left in a hurry,

But now they had a different worry.
What was the name of their hotel?
How would they find dear Miss Clavel?

"Little girl, would it be a bother
To photograph me with my father?"
But the picture Madeline took

Was the portrait of a crook!

"Hey Madeline, thanks for the assistance!"
Caterina said, running into the distance.

The victims were stunned; then both of them hollered,
But lo and behold,

The thief got collared!

"Gotcha!" said the cop as he seized her.

"And don't forget her accomplice either!"

Miss Clavel was at the court
To file a missing persons report.
"That's the second case I've heard today,
Of children who have gone astray.

Their daughter, too, has disappeared.
I'm sad to say, the worst is feared."

In came two criminals, walking slow,
Their noses sniffling, their heads hung low.
What a shameful sign of the time—
Still so young and turned to crime.

"Madeline!" the girls rejoiced
With hugs and cheers and eyes all moist.

"Caterina!" the parents cried.
"When you missed your dinner
we thought you died!"

"Dinner? A home? A FAM-I-LY!"
Said Madeline. "You lied to me!"
"I just wanted to help the cats somehow,"
Caterina said. "What will happen to them now?"
"What's this about some cats I hear?"
Said Poppa. "How many do you have, my dear?"

She'd only made it to eleven
When her momma cried, "Good Heaven!

All of these cats—what shall we do?"
Not a person had a clue
Until Madeline had the inspiration
For how to solve the situation.

First, a complete evacuation!

Then, a rescue operation . . .

An orange tabby was bound for Brazil,

A calico for Notting Hill.

Two more would be meowing Russian.

Off to Stockholm went their cousins.

Cacciopepe, a spotted kitty,
Would make his way to New York City.

Another, missing half his tail,
Was flying home to Israel.

One last cat would be going home
To a beautiful house right here in Rome.

"My parents are letting me keep this one.
Thanks, Madeline, for all you have done."
Her cat let out a happy meow.
And now, dear reader, we bid you . . .

CIAO!